SPIRITUALITY

SPIRITUAL PATH

AMRUTHA PHALA VALLI

Made with ♥ on the Notion Press Platform
www.notionpress.com

THIS BOOK IS DEDICATED TO MY PARENTS AS THEY FOLLOWED THE SPIRITUALITY

I thank my teachers, associations and the books for making me reach the goal. Master Varun has attended many programmes conducted by the foundation and taken notes on this subject. his keen interest in the subject has enabled him to formulate the ideas.

FOSTERING UNIVERSAL UNDERSTANDING

Often people who take responsibility do not pray and those who pray do not take responsibility. But people who take the responsibility of the entire world do pray every day. That is the need of the hour. Every religion has three aspects values, symbols and practices. There is diversity in the practices and symbols, whereas the values are common to all religions. The growth of fanaticism, intolerance and fundamentalism in the world today is because people are only stuck in practices, symbols and customs. They forget about the values (human values). It is very heart touching to see spiritual leaders from all communities to foster human values.

The spirit loves diversity!

There is not just one type of fruit, one type of person or one type of animal all around the world. The spirit loves diversity. Lets not confine the spirit to a uniform. Let's enjoy the diverse variant in creations by honoring, respecting and really loving all of it.

We have often used the term 'religious toleration' earlier. I think these words have become obsolete now. You only tolerate that which you don't love. Don't you think so? The time has come to love

each other's religion as one's own. A religion is great, not because its 'mine' it is great because of what it is. This understanding in all priests, clergymen and those who lead people towards the spiritual and religious light, will put an end to the fanaticism and fundamentalism present in our beautiful world.

It would be very nice if we all together adopt a resolution to educate our people about every religion, so that they have a broader vision of life. No doubt, one must go deep into one's own religion, but at the same time having an understanding about every religion is essential today. We all need to work towards this.

When we pray we see the divinity within us. Without prayer and meditation which are spiritual aspects of life, religion just becomes a dry skin. It's often said that religion is the banana skin and spirituality is the banana. There is misery in the whole world because we throw away the banana and hold on to the dry skin. We need to enhance the spiritual aspects of our lives.

See love inside you that is meditation

See love in the person next to you that is service

Service and meditation go hand in hand.

SPIRITUALITY IS NOTHING OUT OF THIS WORLD

Thinking about God, you will think that you can do idiotic things in your life and with a prayer everything will be fixed. This is not becoming spiritual. It is only when you you become conscious that you will also die then you will turn spiritual. Only when this awareness of mortality seeps into you, you will turn inwards. You will develop the longing to know what this is all about and what is beyond this thing. It will become a natural quest. That is the spiritual process.

The path of any prayer is to be in amazement, to look at the cosmos and say, "wow there are so many planets! So many stars! How big is this universe!" then your consciousness expands and that is meditation.

Creation and creator are not separate. the creator creation is one and the same. The creation is formed out of creator, just like dance comes out of the dancer.

Billions of years have passed since existence began on the earth. Compared to this the span of human life 80 yrs. or 100 yrs. is nothing. In this vast space, where are we?

Seeing yourself in the context of the big creation shifts you to a different level of consciousness. As per one of the scriptures in ancient India There are almost 112 ways of realizing consciousness. One of them is to observe the sky on a clear day...let go and relax. Wherever the mind goes, it makes an assumption. it assumes space and becomes quieter.

Slowly as science is advancing, our perception of what is alive and what is not is changing. Now we know that not just the plants and animals but the rock and soil are alive. The air alive, the water is alive, the soil you walk upon is alive and the very cosmic space is alive. Today science proclaims that water has its own memory and intelligence. One day when science goes far enough, they will find out that there is nothing in the cosmos that is not alive.

People are not entities; they are wave functioning or wave lengths. Just close your eyes and ask yourselves "who am I?" You will get no answer. All you get is space. Once we leave this spirit the mind leaves this body. Once out of the body, the mind cannot be cleansed; it cannot be rid of any thoughts. The body is the instrument or the space where past impression can be washed off.

What Buddha called nirvana, is simply sitting and being in your space, imagining that you are nobody and nothing. When clarity comes, the mind becomes as sharp and powerful as a laser beam. And in that mind an intention fructifies very fast. This mind also has the capacity to heal and elevate itself. Its full of joy, ease and love.

Your entire past is a dream. Just remember all the activities after waking up in the morning. Are they not all like dreams now? In the future in the next 10- 20 years you will be doing many things and they will all pass like dreams. When we go through the process of knowing this and being aware of this the space within us starts to open up and we start experiencing heightened awareness. In fact, a spiritual seeker sitting motionless with eyes closed in deep meditation is contributing to life as much as the politician on the public platform and the scientist in the laboratory. Science strives to bring about happiness to the community by reordering and readjusting things and patterns constituting the world around us. Spirituality strives to bring about a world of perfection through individual perfection; through spiritual values. Science in its inquiry is mainly extrovert and believes that happiness can be brought out from our lives from the world outside.

VAYU

THE PANCHAA PRANAS are in the charge of various activities or process in our body. The first one samana vayu. The samana vayu is in charge of maintaining the temperature of our body. By activating samana vayu we can activate our energies in such a way that we can become less and less available to the external elements in nature. If we go to certain parts of Himalayas, especially if we go to places like Gomukh and Tapovan we will see some sadhus living there in extreme cold in bare minimum clothing. These are glacial, sub- zero temperature areas, but these sadhus can be found walking around bare foot. This is because by doing certain kriyas or mastering certain mantras we can activate the samana vayu and create a kavacha or shield around ourselves.

Generating heat in the body is one aspect of samana vayu, but it is also very healing in nature. If our samana vayu is high, our very presence becomes healing for others. Samana vayu is also in charge of our digestive process. If samana vayu is high, we can notice that whatever we eat digests in an hour. So yogis always want to keep their stomach empty. An empty stomach does not mean you starve yourself. You just burn up the food as quickly as possible.

The next aspect of prana is called Prana Vayu which is in charge of our respiratory process and our thought process. If we carefully observe for every kind of thoughts, we get our breath change in a subtle way. If we sit here and think about the ocean our way of breath will change in a subtle way. If we think about mountains it will be in another way. Think about a tiger it will be yet another way. The reason why thought and respiration are so directly connected are simply because both of these are handled by the same energy called prana vayu. Prana vayu is related to the earth. It is earthy in nature. This is the only planet in solar system to have a breathable atmosphere and therefore the possibility of respiration.

The next aspect of prana is called Udana vayu. Udana means to fly. We may weigh 70-80kg on a weighing scale but we don't feel the weight on us because udana vayu creates buoyancy and make us less available to gravity. There are Yogic practices to obtain this. There were whole schools of Udana vayu in China, where those who gained mastery over this Prana could float around a little bit. We see in movies a little exaggerated. But the body becomes lighter because of a more buoyant force in the body. They have defined gravity simply by creating more buoyancy within the body. If we have complete mastery over udana then we can also fly. But more importantly if we activate our udana we become less and less available to gravity.

The next aspect of prana is called Apana Vayu. Apana vayu is in charge of our excretory system and the sensory function. Only when the excretory system is efficient at the cellularmeans level we will have the necessary sensitivity for sensory perception. And hence such important is being given to the purificatory aspect in yoga. Excretion means not just the outcome of digestion, but excretion on the cellular level that need to happen. Every moment the cells are pushing out impurities at the cellular level. This excretory system will be efficient only when the stomach is empty. When there is food in the stomach and digestion is in progress, the excretory system slows down. So if excretion does not happen properly, the body becomes impure, lethargy and other kind of dullness will settle. Once this inertia manifests in the body, it will slowly be transmitted to the mind also. So Apana vayu cleanses the system in a big way.

The next aspect of prana is Vyana vayu. Vyana vayu is that which knits all these billions of cells into one organism. There have been certain instances of certain yogis whose bodies do not show any signs of decay for months after their death even though no preservation was attempted. This is particularly common in Tibetan monks.This is possible because when they die they leave a certain amount of Vyana prana in the body which preserves it for a long time.

There are many more aspects to pranas or vayus. But fundamentally this is how they effect the physical body. A basic understanding of the pranas is necessary to understand how death happens because at the moment of death, each of these prana recedes differently and effects dead differently.The process of death or the process of disembodiment extends well beyond the point where the breath has stopped.

MEMORY

If we want to understand fundamentally how life and death works, we need to understand how creation works on the role played by the various memories that are present in creation. When we say memory it's not only what we remember but also runs much deeper in its many layers. According to yogic system memory is basically an accumulation of impressions. Further there are eight types of memory in this creation.

ELEMENTARY MEMORY: The most fundamental of these is the elementary memory. According to Yogic system, the first step from unmanifest to manifest is the formation of PANCHA BHOOTAS or the five elements. These elements are prithvi(earth), jal(water), agni(fire), vayu(air) and aakash(ether). These fundamental elements have different characteristics and are manifest in all type of creations. Elementary memory is the memory that decides how these five elements interact and play in life.

ATOMIC MEMORY: Today every child is taught about atomic theory in school. The word atom comes from Greek word atomos meaning indivisible. When modern science discovered the atom, it was believed that atoms were indivisible and most fundamental building block of the universe. Today of course we know that it is not so. Over two dozen subatomic particles have been discovered and more are possible. Atomic memory relates to how subatomic particles, atoms and molecules of various substances are made and how they behave. Elementary memory and atomic memory together constitute what can be called as inanimate memory. This memory governs the inanimate aspect of life. The other types of memory relate to animate life and can be called animate memory.

EVOLUTIONARY MEMORY: Of these the most fundamental layer of memories is evolutionary memory which relates to how the evolution of life has taken place. This is instrumental in you having two eyes, two hands taking the shape of human form and not any other creature and so on.

GENETIC MEMORY: Upon the evolutionary memory comes the genetic memory which comes from the genetic material passed on by our parents that makes us a unique human being that we are among all other humans. This memory decides the color of the skin shape of the body and so on.

KARMIC MEMORY: This is accumulation of all the impressions that we have gathered not just since birth but also from previous lives. And the process of evolution. This will playout in our lives in so many ways beyond ones understanding.

CHAKRAS

The pranic system in the body comprises various energy channels and their points of intersection known as chakras. In Sanskrit, the word "chakra" means "disk" or "wheel" and refers to the energy centers in your body. These wheels or disks of spinning energy each correspond to certain nerve bundles and major organs. To function at their best, your chakras need to stay open, or balanced. If they get blocked, you may experience physical or emotional symptoms related to a particular chakra.

There are seven main chakras that run along your spine. They start at the root, or base, of your spine and extend to the crown of your head. That said, some people believe you have at least 114 different chakras in the body.

The chakras most often referred to are the seven main ones that we'll explore in more detail below.

Root chakra

The root chakra, or Muladhara, is located at the base of your spine. It provides you with a base or foundation for life, and it helps you feel grounded and able to withstand challenges. Your root chakra is responsible for your sense of security and stability.

Sacral chakra

The sacral chakra, or Svadhisthana, is located just below your belly button. This chakra is responsible for your sexual and creative energy. It's also linked to how you relate to your emotions as well as the emotions of others.

Solar plexus chakra

The solar plexus chakra, or Manipura, is located in your stomach area. It's responsible for confidence and self-esteem, as well as helping you feel in control of your life.

Heart chakra

The heart chakra, or Anahata, is located near your heart, in the center of your chest. It comes as no surprise that the heart chakra is all about our ability to love and show compassion.

Throat chakra

The throat chakra, or Vishuddha, is located in your throat. This chakra has to do with our ability to communicate verbally.

Third eye chakra

The third eye chakra, or Ajna, is located between your eyes. You can thank this chakra for a strong gut instinct. That's because the third eye is responsible for intuition. It's also linked to imagination.

Crown chakra

The crown chakra, or Sahasrara, is located at the top of your head. Your Sahasrara represents your spiritual connection to yourself, others, and the universe. It also plays a role in your life's purpose.

Function & Importance of the Chakras

The chakras are the distribution centers. They distribute the five pranas to their local regions. Each chakra is located in a specific region and it caters to that region. For example, the root chakra will distribute the Apana prana and distribute it to the pelvic region providing energy for the organs in the pelvic region. When a chakra is not functioning properly, this distribution gets disturbed and physical or energetical issues arise.

What is the shape of a Chakra?

There are many myths about the shape of the chakras. Some say that chakras are like whirling discs, some believe chakras are like flowers hanging from the spine, some think that chakras are like ice cream cones. The confusion is there because the chakras can not be seen by the eyes or by any device. So, we believe what we have heard. Now the ancient scripture say that a chakra is a sphere, like a ball. Earth is a major chakra of our solar system and a minor chakra for the galaxy milky way. It rotates to distribute some energy which is beyond human imagination.

Where are Chakras located?

The chakras are located in the spinal cord in the astral body. The astral body is the energy body residing inside the physical body. Every physical body part has a corresponding astral body part. The astral body can not be seen or touched. This is also a reason why we cannot see the chakras.

What is the size of a Chakra?

Some people say that chakras are one foot in radius, some say that they change their size according to the energy flow. But scriptures tell us that the chakras are very small, as they are located in the astral spinal cord which is located inside the physical spinal cord.

How to balance or awaken your seven Chakras

Every chakra rotates at a specific frequency and speed. This frequency and speed can change due to various factors like diet, lifestyle, thought patterns, etc. This results in issues with the distribution of the pranas. Imagine if your 50 watt light bulb getting a 500 watt or 10-watt electricity supply. When we say balance or awaken the chakras, we mean to bring to chakra back to its regular speed.

Some of the tools to balance the chakras are:

Diet: One of the main reasons for imbalance in chakras is an imbalance of the five elements in the body. A balanced diet helps to bring balance in the elements of the body.

Asanas: asanas help to stimulate chakras to improve their functioning and heal themselves.

Breathing: breathing helps to increase the flow of prana in the body and remove stale prana.

Meditation: Meditation helps to clear the mind and remove negativity and manipulation.

KARMA

Karma represents the ethical dimension of the process of rebirth (samsara), belief in which is generally shared among the religious traditions of India. Indian soteriology (theories of salvation) posit that future births and life situations will be conditioned by actions performed during one's present life—which itself has been conditioned by the accumulated effects of actions performed in previous lives. The doctrine of karma thus directs adherents of Indian religions toward their common goal: release (moksha) from the cycle of birth and death. Karma thus serves two main functions within Indian moral philosophy: it provides the major motivation to live a moral life, and it serves as the primary explanation of the existence of evil.

Although there are many types of karma, the Vedas and Upanishads only speak of the four main ones.

Prarabdha Karma or Matured Karma. When we do something, it is taken note of by the universe. ...

Sanchita Karma or Stored Karma. ...

Agami Karma or Forthcoming Karma. ...

Vartamana Karma or Present Karma.

Prarabdha Karma are the part of sanchita karma, a collection of past karmas, which are ready to be experienced through the present body. According to Sri Swami Sivananda: "Prarabdha is that portion of the past karma which is responsible for the present body.

In Hinduism, sanchita karma (heaped together) is one of the three kinds of karma. It is the sum of one's past karmas — all actions, good and bad, from one's past lives follow through to the next life.

Agami Karma is the Karma we are creating for ourselves right here in the current moment. It is the action that we create and the choices we make right now, as we live this present lifetime. All these three aspects of karma blend into each other.

Vartamana or Present Karma

This karma is also known as kriyamāṇa, and represents the actionable, present karma, which is true to the moment. This allows you to change your decisions on a regular basis which will affect only the present. Sometimes, life offers you to make decisions for yourself.

VEDAS

Any of the four collections forming the earliest body of Indian scripture, consisting of the Rig Veda, Sama Veda, Yajur Veda, and Atharva Veda, which codified the ideas and practices of Vedic religion and laid down the basis of classical Hinduism. They were probably composed between 1500 and 700 BC, and contain hymns, philosophy, and guidance on ritual The Vedas, meaning "knowledge," are the oldest texts of Hinduism. They are derived from the ancient Indo-Aryan culture of the Indian Subcontinent and began as an oral tradition that was passed down through generations before finally being written in Vedic Sanskrit.

The Vedas teach us to pursue truth, to accept nothing but the Truth, which is one, though the wise describe it in various ways: ekam sat viprāh bahudhā vadanti. That Truth or sat is synonymous with being and becoming, with life and living in all its manifestations.

RIG VEDA

According to the Puranic tradition, Ved Vyasa compiled all the four Vedas, along with the Mahabharata and the Puranas. Vyasa then taught the Rigveda samhita to Paila, who started the oral tradition.

The Vedas teach us to pursue truth, to accept nothing but the Truth, which is one, though the wise describe it in various ways: ekam sat viprāh bahudhā vadanti. ... The countless forms of creation manifest the Truth or Reality of God or Brahman, which is variously imagined, described and named. The Rig-Veda contains 1,028 mantras, or hymns, directed to the gods and natural forces. The mantras are organized into ten books called mandalas, or circles. According to ancient Hindu tradition, the mantras were based on divine revelations received by members of a particular family.

SAMA VEDA

The Sama Veda represents the force of spiritual knowledge and the power of devotion. The book was revealed to Vayu rishi. It consists hymns of the Rigveda put to a musical measure. Hence the text of the Sama Veda is an alternative version of the Rig Veda. Sama Veda is an ancient Hindu Vedic Scripture. It is one of the four main Vedas of Hinduism. It contains a collection of melodies and chants. Sama means "melody," and Veda means "knowledge." Samaveda has been described as the "Book of Song" or "The Veda of Chants" or even as the "Yoga of Song."

YAJUR VEDA

The Yajurveda is the Veda primarily of prose mantras for worship rituals. An ancient Vedic Sanskrit text, it is a compilation of ritual-offering formulas that were said by a priest while an individual performed ritual actions such as those before the yajna fire.

ATHARVA VEDA

The Atharvaveda is a collection of 20 books, with a total of 730 hymns of about 6,000 stanzas. The Atharva Veda is a Vedic-era collection of spells, prayers, charms, and hymns. There are prayers to protect crops from lightning and drought, charms against venomous serpents, love spells, healing spells, hundreds of verses, some derived from the Rig Veda, all very ancient.

The Atharva Veda is deemed to be an encyclopaedia for medicine "Interalia", and Ayurveda (the science of life) is considered as Upa Veda (supplementary subject) of the Atharva Veda.

In spiritual way vedas are the roots of knowledge. The four vedas contain full knowledge in all the fields.

YOGA

What is Yoga, exactly? Is it just an exercise form? Is it a religion, a philosophy, an ideology? Or is it something else entirely? The word "Yoga" literally means "union". In this article, Sadhguru offers the following Yoga definition; essentially, "that which brings you to reality."

The moment you attach the word "Yoga," it indicates it is a complete path by itself. Literally, it means "union." Union means it brings you to the ultimate reality, where individual manifestations of life are surface bubbles in the process of creation. Right now, a coconut tree and a mango tree have popped up from the same earth. From the same earth, the human body and so many creatures have popped up. It is all the same earth.

Yoga means to move towards an experiential reality where one knows the ultimate nature of the existence, the way it is made.

Initially, Yoga was imparted by the Adiyogi (the first yogi), Shiva, over 15,000 years ago. It was Adiyogi who introduced to humanity the idea that one can evolve beyond one's present level of existence. He poured his knowing into the legendary Sapta Rishis, or seven sages, who took the tremendous possibility offered by the yogic science to various parts of the world, including Asia, ancient Persia, northern Africa, and South America. It is this fundamental yet sophisticated science of elevating human consciousness that is the source of the world's spiritual traditions, predating religion by many thousands of years. Yoga is about attaining absolute Balance, piercing Clarity, and an inexhaustible Exuberance. With this, you are immensely fit for life.

The name "8 Limbs" comes from the Sanskrit term Ashtanga and refers to the eight limbs of yoga: Yama (attitudes toward our environment), Niyama (attitudes toward ourselves), Asana (physical postures), Pranayama (restraint or expansion of the breath), Pratyahara (withdrawal of the senses), Dharana (concentration), Dhyana (meditation) and Samadhi (complete integration). At 8 Limbs Yoga Centers our drop-in classes focus on asana and pranayama. We also offer classes on other aspects to guide practitioners on their path: check out our Workshops and Deepening Series. Our Teacher Training Programs are not only to learn to teach yoga, but to guide the dedicated practitioner further on their path through accountability and community.

Yoga's benefits affect each person in a different way. Many find that it helps them to relax; others find themselves feeling healthier and more energetic. All the systems in the body-from the lymphatic to the digestive to the cardiovascular-benefit from yoga. Yoga benefits every aspect of our bodies, inside and out.

On the inside, yoga enables relaxation. Many practitioners find that yoga helps them to focus and feel relaxed in both work and play. In 2003, scientists studied both long-time yogis and beginners; they found that the stress hormone cortisol had decreased, even after just one session of yoga. Yoga has also been found to increase alpha and theta waves in the brain, meaning that yoga can relax the brain and increase access to the subconscious and emotions. And by simply increasing the feel-good brain chemicals like endorphins, enkephalins, and serotonin, yoga practitioners just feel better.

On the outside, yogis look terrific. This is probably from improvements on the inside! Since yoga balances the metabolism and provides exercise, many find yoga brings their body into balance. Physical yoga strengthens and tones the muscles while improving balance and posture. And yoga is a great way to cross-train for other sports; it can ease strains from injuries and increase strength and flexibility.

When all the body's systems are balanced, yoga practitioners feel healthier and find they want to make other healthy choices in their life.

BRANCHES OF YOGA

Hatha Yoga is the physical practice of yoga. The asana practice of hatha yoga symbolizes the connection of the sun and the moon, bringing the world and the physical body into balance. Hatha also means "to strike," meaning to strike the body with the challenge of the postures and to "yoke" (the meaning of yoga) the mind into singular focus. Most styles of yoga in the United States are based in Hatha with different philosophies, practices, and terminology that allow yoga to fit the individual practitioner. Its traditional source in relation to the postures is the Hatha Yoga Pradipika. See below for more information on styles of Hatha yoga.

Raja Yoga is the Royal Path ("raja" means king), the yoga of meditation. Its focus is to quiet the mind. The practitioner's attention is fixed on an object, mantra, or concept. Whenever the mind wanders it is brought back to the object of concentration. In time the mind will cease wandering and become completely still. Raja yoga practitioners aim to establish "a mental link with the supreme source of all spiritual energy and power, the Supreme Soul, with the purpose of freeing the individual soul from misery, pain, fear, illness, and phobias, and enabling the soul to experience peace, happiness and lasting health and prosperity."

Jnana Yoga is the yoga of knowledge. Jnana yoga is closely associated with Advaita Vedanta, one of the six philosophies of Hinduism. Advaita Vedanta believes that everything in the universe shares a single soul, including all living creatures and God. Jnana yoga is the wisdom associated with discerning the Real from the unreal or illusory.

Bhakti Yoga is the yoga of devotion. In Bhakti yoga, the practitioner's emotional force is concentrated and channeled toward the Divine. Bhakti practitioners are openly expressive; their devotion is sometimes compared to a love-relationship with a divine being. Kirtan, devotional singing, is a popular practice of Bhakti yoga.

Karma Yoga is the yoga of service to others and to God. Karma yoga practitioners renounce the fruits of action. Activities are assumed for the benefit of the greater good, without concern for personal benefit. The path of Karma-Yoga is described in detail in the Bhagavad-Gita: "Be intent on action; not on the fruits of action."

MEDITATION

The definition of meditation is mental activity in relation to Brahma in the form of Iswara. Vyapara means any activity. It is qualified by the word "manasa" meaning mental. Whenever a word is qualified by an adjective there should be a need for it. If meditation is an activity qualified by the word mental it negates all physical activities from its purview. However, it implies other activities belonging to the same group. Any thinking is a mental activity. Sadness is also a mental activity, as it is a mental expression of one's emotion. In dream also one will always be in meditation, because there is a lot of mental activity in dream.

Let's now look into the visible results of meditation. In order to understand the visible effects of meditation, we need some insight into the nature of mind. The mind is always busy and its nature is restless. In Gita Arjuna says "I can perhaps stop the wind with my hand but not the mind" mind itself is restlessness. The mind is entrenched, turbulent and very powerful. How then can one sit and meditate?

The nature of mind is like a movie film. In a movie the camera will always be moving. Since the film is moving with a certain speed, it can record the motion. Similarly, when anyone moves their hand you are able to record and recognize its motion. This implies that mental frame is also changing to keep up with motion.

When you look into the nature of thinking, it's very interesting to observe how the mind moves from one object to another. There are so many simultaneous tracks and nobody knows how the mind is going to land upon the next thought. For example, if you walk out and see a car, a Mercedes Benz, It draws your attention, You think of Germany, you think of Hitler, Thinking of Hitler you inevitably become depressed. Your mind travels from Benz to Germany, Germany to Hitler, Hitler to holocaust and so on. The whole line of thinking emerged from just seeing a car.

Thinking is the privilege of a human being. However, it can become a problem, because thinking can often lead to worry and depression. You cannot become worried or sad without thinking. In deep sleep you are not sad as you don't think. Similarly, without thinking you cannot be angry. Angry happens when one does not want to be angry.

Undeniably, a mere physical body will not move or act unless the life principle is found enriched in it. The life Centre in each one of us is sacred spot from which all activities emanate. Without that life factor visualizing the body, the mind and the intellect, you will be nothing but inert matter unable to read, analyze and understand these words. This divine spark of life is called atman in Vedanta and is considered to be enveloped by layers of matter of varying degree of grossness. The outermost shell the grossest is the body. And almost all throughout our consciousness we go about considering ourselves to be only this body.

Composition of various sheaths is as follows.

1. Food sheath: The physical body of which everyone is still aware during the waking stage of consciousness is called food sheath. Its born of food assimilated by the parents, it exists because of the food regularly taken in, and ultimately after death it must decompose to form food again. The physical structure, which arises from food, exists in food and go back to food is most appropriately called the food sheath.(ANNAMAYA KOSHA)

2. Vital- Air sheath: The air we breathe mixes with the blood and reaches every cell of the body. Oxygen forms an inner lining as it were for the outer physical sheath. The vital air sheath controls all the organs of action and it is fivefold with five different functions. Prana, Apana, samana vyana, udana which makes it possible for people to entertain, absorb and eliminate thoughts. (MANOMAYA KOSHA)

3. Mental sheath: None of us is unaware of the existence of the mind. The mind entertains our doubts, joy, and a variety of emotions and constantly erupts with a non-stop flow of thought lava. The mind can fly to things and places seen or heard. (PRANAMAYA KOSHA)

4. Intellectual sheath: When the mind is the doubting element, the intellect is the determining factor in each of us. In Vedantic literature both are considered one and the same. When a thought arises at a determined decision or a willed judgement they are called intellect. The intellect is subtler than the mind because it ventures forth into realms, unheard and unseen. Realms not experienced are fields of revelry and conquest. The mind and intellect together are known as the subtle- body. (VIGNANAMAYA KOSHA)

5. Bliss sheath: This, the subtle of the sheaths is made up of ignorance that exists during our deep sleep state of consciousness. It is considered blissful because we experience a state of pure non-apprehension that is the absence of everything. This sheath is called the casual body. (ANANDAMAYA KOSHA)

THE GROSS BODY

A stone is unaware of the external world of circumstances. Plants are not aware of any inner world of thoughts; animals though aware of the external world and the mental zone, are not conscious of their intellect. The human being is the only animal that is, to a comparatively greater degree, at once conscious of the world outside and world within. That is, he is the only being who has developed mental and intellectual faculties. The attempt to the seeker is to develop the awareness to such an extent that he or she becomes aware of not only the outer and inner worlds but also of the innermost spirit. The rishis considering the human being as the one endowed with the greatest manifestation of awareness, closely analyzed the grades of consciousness through which he or she lives. They codified their exhaustive study and defined the three states of consciousness. The waking state; the dream state and the deep sleep state

The gross body, consisting of the food and the vital air sheaths, is the platform from which we look out into the world where sense objects are made available for our cognition The state of conscious is called the waking state. The mind and the intellect together constitute the subtle body, identifying with which we look into an inner world of experiences. This state is known as the dream state. When we have withdrawn from waking state and have also folded up our dream world, we are in the state of deep sleep, in which we identify ourselves with the bliss sheath, called the casual body by the seers.

We have already found that each one of us consists of multiple personalities, and that we judge the world of things and circumstances differently according to the particular personality functioning in us at a given moment. That which we may accept as a ideal state of things from the stand point of the physical being may not be acceptable to our psychological being.

MIND

In all religions we have a necessity to control our mind. Mind is thought flow just as water flowing in a given direction is a river, so thoughts flowing continuously from individual to the world of objects is the mind. The character of a river is determined by the character of water. If water is bad the river will not be good. In the same way the thoughts arising in the mind determines the state of mind. The quality of thoughts in our mind depends on the type of objects that initiate or sustain our thoughts. The company of good people, dynamic aspirational and inspirational ideals all these change the life pattern. A river with floods and flowing with high velocity cannot be controlled similar is the state of mind. A quite mind is available for remodeling.

The removal of unwanted lumber, dust and cobwebs is but half the process of making the deserted house habitable once again. Spirituality is the technique you need to accomplish this change. Actual achievement must be proceeded by firm determination. Once begun this process gathers momentum; thereafter constant vigilance ensures smooth transformation

Ordinarily The mind is active. It is its nature to be forever unsteady. It cannot remain a moment, without entertaining one thought after another. If mind functions exclusively in a given field it becomes highly potent in the given field. We saw how we can order the mind to halt its chanting, leaving its only field of occupation at that moment. In the moment of vital silence that follows, the mind is at its most dynamic though compared to our ordinary mis understand this silent moment of extreme dynamism as an impotent interval of emptiness' or of nonexistence.

When good and bad meet face to face, tension and activity are always present. It is an eternal law. We can never mentally get away from these two opposing forces, and when we identify with them we suffer consequent dispassion. At one moment we identify with the good in us, and feel unhappy because in spite of ourselves, we feel tempted to act in a vicious, negative way. The following method can be employed to gain control over the mind.

1. Bring the mind back forcefully
2. Be conscious about what you are doing
3. Chant with eyes open
4. Give the mind a large but inspiring field to pay in

DEATH

Do we know we all die one day? We cannot be sure with other things in our life. We don't know whether we will get married or not whether we get job or not; whether we will be successful in life but one thing is sure that we all are going to die. Each second two people die in the world. One day everyone is going to die.

In the Indian tradition, cremation grounds are always held to be very sacred. If someone dies even if it is someone you don't know, it hits you somewhere. In any genuine spiritual practice, there is always the smell of death. If we go deep enough into it, it will remind us that we are mortal. Traditionally, every yogi started his spiritual pursuit in the cremation grounds, in fact many masters have used this as spiritual process. Gautama The Buddha made it compulsory for his monks. Before he initiated anyone who came to him he asked them to go and sit in the cremation grounds for three months, just watching the corpses burning. Death is a very fundamental question. Actually death is very closer to us than the statistics we read about it. Each moment death is happening in us at the organ and cellular levels. Only if we are ignorant and unaware does it seem like death will come to you someday later. If we are aware we will see both life and death are happening every moment. Upon birth, the first thing the child does is to inhale *and the last thing we will do in our life is exhalation.*

People think that death is a tragedy. It is not. People living their entire life without experiencing life is a tragedy. If you die, there is really no tragedy. If you die, there is really no tragedy. That is the end of all the problems you face in life but if you are alive and not experiencing life in its totality, that is a true tragedy.

No two people in the world live their lives the same way. Similarly, no two people die the same way. People may die in the same situation of the same cause, but still they don't do the same way. Being able to raise the dead is a deep fascination for most people. For them that is the ultimate rest of someone's spiritual powers. Most people are living like the dead anyway because they are unconscious of many things within themselves. If people are living unconsciously, it is as good as death. So in a way the whole spiritual process is about raising the death.

Suicide: Ones whole life is like a penance. One's whole life is like a frying pan! We are bothered by everything. We are bothered by people we hate and we are also bothered by people we love! Actually the people we love are bigger botheration to us than the people we hate.

Life is like a frying pan. Don't jump into fire from the frying pan. Face life. Don't escape from it. Escaping from life is directly jumping into fire because there is no escape from life. People commit suicide, thinking they will be able to escape life but they are 'jumping into fire and this is more horrible. It's not the solution, Its ignorance. Suicide is more among capable people. They feel a dryness inside, an emptiness. Support needs to come from within. It's not just food and water that's needed. Spiritual strength is what is needed. It is spiritual that can build vacuum in our life. Suicidal rates and depression are also increasing because the value of doing is not being addressed. In order to get satisfaction in life we need to do some form of service which increases the confidence level.

SPIRITUALITY

Q. What is the spiritual path?

A. Love, joy, bliss, compassion, beauty and enthusiasm all are made up of spirit. Enlivening these is spirituality. To grow in unconditional love and in beauty is spirituality. Freedom is the nature of our spirit. Being centered and being calm is meditation.

Q. What is the difference between Spirituality and religion?

A. Spirituality is flesh of banana and religion the peel. Don't hold on to the peel and throw away the real stuff. Religion and its significance is the essence of spirituality.

Q Why is spirituality the only way to true happiness and joy?

A. Spirituality means you are not just this body, nor this mind. You are the spirit. Just as the body and mind have their own food, the spirit has its own too. The food of spirituality is love, joy, compassion and beauty. Spirituality is honoring the truth. Spirituality gives you strength; that inner to manage difficult situations and always makes you smile.

Q Do spiritual and material advancements block each other?

A. If you are advancing spiritually, it does not block you from material advancements. In ancient INDIA spiritual and material advancements were never considered antagonistic but were considered complementary

Q What is success?

A. Success cannot be computed by the money and power you have. A smile that comes from inside heart, which feels freedom in life is the sign of success. When there is a feverish for success, it shows a lack of confidence. The sign of success is putting 100 percent but not depending on the results is a sign of success. For you to be youthful in spirit, you need to be enthusiastic and open minded not cynical or sarcastic.

Contents

Foreword

Most of us are in bondage of of worldly matters because of spoken words only, like the sweet baby words to the loving dialect to our dear ones. Even enimity is caused by words. The power of words can create endless waves of love and hatred in our mind and heart. Speechless is the engine of spirituality.

Preface

Remember, most of us are like an oak tree in a flower pot. Let this book help you transform the limimting mind. Allow the gardener in you to plant your life in such a way that it would flower into a limitless understanding of life.

Acknowledgements

I thank my parents, teachers and friends in knowing the knowledge given in the book. They encouraged me a lot in preparing the book .

www.ingramcontent.com/pod-product-compliance
Lightning Source LLC
Chambersburg PA
CBHW060219120726
48004CB00008B/1874